Digiboy

Dear Emilka,

I hope you enjoy
my story about Finnd
Digiboy!

Marian Bennam

Copyright

This novel is a work of fiction. The characters and places in the story are the work of the author's imagination.

www.marianbrennan.com

ISBN: 978-1-7399835-3-6
Published by Blackditch Press

Marian Brennan

The Adventures of Finn O'Shea

Book 1

ISBN: 9798566652085

Meet Finn O'Shea… He is smart, he is witty … and he is an **inventor**!

'An inspiring story of courage, determination and resilience.'

iii

The Adventures of Finn O'Shea

Book 2

ISBN: 9781739983505

Join Finn and his friends on a trip to the USA to visit the Space Centre where an unexpected sequence of events takes them on an epic adventure!

Marian Brennan

For Oscar.

Thank You's

To all the inspiring children in my life, this book is for all of you. Thank you for all the delightful feedback from my readers. I love reading your comments. A big thank you to my advanced readers Tom Matthews, Sophia Matthews, Keyaan, Aoife Chubb, Oscar Chubb, Aine-Rose Calverley and Jenny Smith for all your comments and enthusiasm. Thank you to Antonia Prescott for reviewing the draft manuscript and providing insightful comments. Thank you to Anthony for your enthusiastic ongoing support of my writing.

Marian Brennan

Contents

"I loved the way it was a page-turner with something exciting happening on every page. I liked the way they coded and figured out problems, and the amazing plot twist at the end."- Aoife (age 11)

"This is the best book ever! I really like how the dog talks."- Oscar (age 10)

"I like it because it's cool to read especially then bit with the volcano!" -Kieran (age 5)

Chapter 1: Out of control

I was moving fast, the wind whipping against my cheeks. It was cold and dark. I was sliding down a long bendy slide, going faster and faster... The slide bent and dipped without warning. It was pitch, pitch black. So dark I couldn't see my legs. I screamed with every surprising drop, my belly jumping into my throat. I was thrown left and right, then tumbled down to a new level. I was tumbling head over heels out of control bumping against the sides. **"Ouch!"** Immediately the slide turned right and sped up super, super-fast until I was rolling out of the tunnel into bright light.

"Aaagh!" I moaned as the pain from the light seared into my eyes. The tunnel had been so dark and the light on the platform was so bright that my eyes burned. I was blinking and could barely see anything. It reminded me of summertime when my cousins shone their flashlights in my eyes when we were camping.

The platform was quite small with lots of buttons and switches. I really wanted to press them to see what they all did, but that had got me into trouble before, so I waited.

I was tired and hungry and my clothes were ripped from being tumbled and tossed for hours through the tunnels. The platform was like an island in a sea of tunnel connections that exited out in all directions to what seemed like infinity... and beyond! I knew that I needed to choose a tunnel, but I also needed to rest. I also needed a map... This is what one normally used when one was lost, but it may not even have been useful in this situation, as I was not sure where I was trying to go or where I was.

I sat in the middle considering my options and trying to catch my breath! At first, the buttons all looked the same. There were what seemed like a hundred tunnels going off the giant floating platform. All tunnels headed off into the blackness. After the last trip through the tunnel, I was not that keen to get into another one, but there also did not seem to be anything on the platform except buttons and screens on a control panel in the middle. All of a sudden, the light that shone brightly when I had landed on the platform went out. Immediately I felt sorry that I hadn't quickly examined all the buttons more closely before the lights went off.

I felt through my pockets taking an inventory of what was left. I usually had a small torch, some string, a bit of flint and one or two sweets. My mom wouldn't let me have a penknife, otherwise, I would have had that too. I was really hungry and so started to suck on one of the sweets. I felt better straight away and congratulated myself for putting the sweets in my pocket with the zip. If I hadn't, I definitely would have lost them in the tunnels. Although the light from under the platform was still shining, the platform itself was dark and seemed to be floating in a sea of blackness. I fished my torch out of my pocket and tried to switch it on. It did not work! The torch often didn't work, so I shook it and smacked it with my hand and bright light shot out of the bulb as the batteries connected. Now I moved it slowly and gently across the platform to examine all the controls being careful not to step off the edge.

All the tunnels were covered with what looked like a little door. The doors had no handles, and it was not obvious what you needed to do to open them. Nothing was labelled. The buttons looked the same, the tunnels looked the same, so there was no way of knowing which one to pick. I carried on this slow and thorough search of the platform moving from where I had started in a circle around the edge. Then I turned to the middle where there were more buttons on what looked like a control panel.

It was tempting to press the big red button, but I didn't yet dare. I carried on carefully looking at each section slowly. As I examined the control panel, I saw some small letters etched roughly into the plastic next to a square blue button.

It was just one word:

'Digiboy'

"Digiboy!" I said slowly, considering this. Another boy with a penknife had been here I thought. Without thinking anymore, I pressed the button.

Chapter 2: The Beast

The platform disappeared and I was falling in space.

"Aaaaaaaaaaagh!!!" I yelled as I fell through the darkness. An electronic bleep sounded **"bloup, bloup, bloup"** like I'd reached a new level in a video game. I landed on my feet on a new flat platform that was lit up with lights, I was blinking trying to see in the bright light. A loud roar made me run without thinking. As I ran, the path lit up. Run, jump, duck, I didn't have time to think... run, jump, duck, slide... Over a wall, around the corner all the time following the light as fast as I could to get away from the loud running footsteps. I felt the torch fall from my pocket... The breathing behind me was louder... rasping breath! Really, really close behind me. I turned to look and tripped sliding into a dive on my tummy on the glass floor. The beast stepped on me as it carried on running. The beast's claw made a huge gash on my shoulder. I felt warm blood trickle down my back and my front. I ripped some cloth from my already ripped shirt and pressed down on the cut to stop the bleeding. My mom always did this if I had a cut. She always said: "you need to press down to stop the bleeding". She had done this the day I needed stitches after cutting myself with my penknife... the day she took it away. I wished I was home now in my warm house. My shoulder hurt. I rubbed my shirt against my tummy to smear the dribble of blood. The cut was still bleeding. I held the pressure on catching my breath again. "Digiboy," I said to myself. It was very bright. So bright that I could hardly look at the new platform or path that I was on. I got up and started to walk slowly along the path. The beast was gone. I was no longer sure it was even chasing me. Maybe something even bigger was chasing it! That didn't bear thinking about. The road seemed to go on forever. Only blackness on either side. "What is this place?" I thought. I hadn't had any time to think about this strange situation I had found myself in.

I fished in my pocket again and found some small stones. My little sister loved filling my pockets with small stones from the beach. This was normally irritating, and my mum got very cross when they came out in the washing machine.

Now I took one and dropped it over the side of the path. My dad had taught me to test the depth of water with a stick. Now I had the idea of dropping a stone to see how far the drop was next to his path...

'Maybe there was no drop?'

I let the stone go and waited for the sound of it hitting the ground below.

I waited... and waited... and waited.

Nothing. No sound. "Infinity and beyond!" I mumbled to myself. I trundled on placing one foot in front of the other. Counting my steps, singing songs until my legs could no longer move. I sat down to take a break and fell asleep on the hard bright floor.

I woke a few hours later. I had no idea how long I had been asleep. If this was a video game, it was the most boring game I'd ever played. Although, I was actually quite happy it was boring as I was not sure how many more beasts I wanted to meet. I touched my shoulder, checking it wasn't all a dream. The cut was still there and my shoulder was now even more sore than earlier. It couldn't be a dream as I was pretty sure you could not go to sleep and wake up in a dream and you couldn't get hurt in dreams!

If this was a computer game, then I would need to get to the next level. It seemed like I was maybe in a broken game, or the back end of the game ...and who was Digiboy?

I walked on in a forward direction, as there seemed no point in going back. The path had no obstacles only an alternating pattern of black and white blocks. I started playing hopscotch to amuse myself. All the while I was singing "Digiboy, Digiboy where is the next clue?" "Digiboy, Digiboy, I am gonna find you." I started to hear trickling water. It seemed strange in this digital world that there might be a river, as water and electronics do not mix. I wasn't sure which direction the water was coming from. It was soft at first but started getting louder as I walked. The air got colder and I felt small droplets on my skin, a bit like when you are at the beach and the waves are crashing nearby. I also started to smell something. The smell after the rain comes, a muddy smell? No. It was wet dog! Wet dog I pondered. How strange! I did not have a dog and had become a bit scared of dogs recently as a little dog had chased me and nipped at my ankles. I became a little nervous, "what if this was another beast or an even bigger beast?"

my heart beat faster and I breathed deeply trying to calm myself down. My legs felt heavy as I trudged on.

After a while, I started to hear a soft whimpering sound. It didn't sound like a beast. I looked around carefully, the water was running next to the path now and a little dog was clinging onto the edge exhausted.

Without thinking whether the dog was friend or foe, I grabbed it by the shoulders and pulled it up. The dog was shaggy and shaking uncontrollably with the cold. I immediately wrapped my arms around the dog to warm him up. This made me cold, wet and smelly, but the dog stopped shaking.

In fact, after a while, the dog became so still that I wondered whether the dog had died! I put my finger below the dog's nostrils and felt warm breath coming out. The dog was not dead; he had just gone to sleep.

Chapter 3: Talking dogs & other oddities!

I lay there quite still wrapped around my new friend trying to understand what was going on. There were three options the first was to keep going forwards, the second was to go backwards, and the third was to go swimming in the rushing water. There was no point going backwards unless I wanted to try one of the tunnels.

The dog was completely exhausted, so swimming was probably not the best plan. I decided, therefore, to try going forwards for a short while and if nothing interesting happened, I would go back to the tunnel platform. Although I wasn't actually sure I could get back to it now.

The dog was a small sausage dog and I decided to call him Cosmay or Cosie for short. It was a joke for myself about the cosmic experience I seemed to be having. It was lucky the dog was small or else I would not have been able to carry him and keep going. I walked for another kilometre or so until I couldn't feel my arms anymore from the dog's weight and finally sat down to rest. My legs were so weak that I could no longer go on. The dog blinked its eyes, waking up and licked my face softly.

"Thank you for saving me," he said.

Now I thought I was dreaming.

"You can talk?" I asked.

"Of course," the dog said. "All dogs can talk."

"Most of us just choose not to."

"Can I call you Cosie?" I asked.

"Sure. Dogs don't have names generally, it is humans that give us names, so you can call me whatever you want."

"How did you get here?" I asked.

"How did you get here?" asked the dog.

"Well, you see, I don't really know, and I'm not sure what I'm supposed to do to get home and I'm starting to get really hungry."

"Well, I don't know what you are doing here or how you can get out, but I can normally smell which way to go to find food."

And so, the friendship began, Cosie and me in it together, and now it did not feel half as hard. We walked on until we came to a junction point. The path split into what seemed like spaghetti! Narrow paths bent and twisted up and down and all around like some sort of tangled spaghetti junction. There was no way to know which way to go. Cosie suggested he run ahead a few meters onto each path and sniff to see if he could smell any food smells. He ran in and out, backwards and forwards and after the fifth tunnel, I heard him bark. I followed him down the path suggested by the barking.

"Why are you barking if you can talk?" I asked.

"Because it is louder, and I quite enjoy barking!" said Cosie.

Cosie had found them what seemed like a real live game inside a game where you could find food!

We ran in different directions. It seemed like a giant maze where there was food hanging from the hedges that we could just pick off. It was super easy, until I realised that there was something chasing us! I could hear the raspy breathing again and realised there were monsters and beasts trying to catch us. I was not sure what would happen if they caught us, so I ran really fast ducking and diving, and changing direction. I lost Cosie and my bearings, but gained a bunch of grapes, an apple, some cherries, chocolate and a banana. As I reached the banana, I could feel the breath of a monster on the back of my neck.

The monster chased me and I could smell

its disgusting breath as I got to the middle of the maze. Instantaneously, the monster and all the walls disappeared. Cosie appeared right next to me with a sausage in his mouth. We sat down panting and feasted on our spoils. Never had grapes and bananas tasted so good. I kept the cherries, apple and chocolate bar for later.

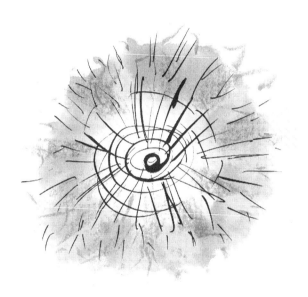

Chapter 4: Let's Play this Game

"What now?" asked Cosie.

I prided myself on always being very logical and strategic.

"Well," I said, "We are in a very good position. We have eaten and have some extra food. We have won the last game and we have both had some sleep and there are two of us."

"Yeh. As far as games go, we are powered up and we haven't lost any lives," said Cosie.

"I think I'd prefer if we tried not to lose any lives in case we only have our one life," I said.

While we were philosophising about the game, the game had something else in mind for us.

"Whoa!" I exclaimed.

"What now?!?!?"

The path had simply disappeared. Now we were standing at the end of a long platform looking down into an abyss of empty space. The platform was wider than the path, but still really quite narrow. We stood there in disbelief looking at the void and then back at each other. "It's a really long way back now", said Cosie.

Suddenly, giant blocks started appearing all around us.

"Let's play this game!" I said, determined to beat the game.

I started stacking blocks as fast as I could, building a tall tower. Quickly it was taller than me, so I started building a spiral staircase around the edge of the tower. I ran up and down collecting blocks, building the tower and then adding to the staircase as I went. The blocks just kept appearing, and I kept building.

Cosie couldn't help with this task as he was a dog and his paws were no help at all.

"Do you think we are going up a level?" he asked.

I was so out of breath I could hardly answer.

"We have to keep building or these blocks will push us off the platform!"

We had gone up about 10 meters and I was exhausted. Finally, the blocks stopped coming and I collapsed in a heap!

"Now what?" asked Cosie.

"Now we rest," I said.

But again, the game had other plans for us. An angry looking bird appeared.

"Throw it!" shouted Cosie.

"What?" I shouted back.

"Throw it!"

I grabbed the bird and threw it into the blackness. The bird flew back angrier than ever! It was swooping and squawking at us as it flew past.

"Feed it!" shouted Cosie.

"We hardly have any food left," I shouted.

"Try feeding him your cherries," said Cosie. I held up the cherries and the bird snatched them out of my hand gulping them all in one go.

The bird doubled in size and carried on swooping and squawking at us.

"Got any other bright ideas?" I shouted as I got a peck on the head.

A bright platform lit up in the distance. Throw him again towards the green light.

I grabbed the bird's feet and started to spin the bird in a circle and then launched the bird towards the platform. The bird landed on the platform and disappeared. I was exhausted again and sat down crossed legged on the floor panting.

"I'm not sure how much more of this I can take," I said.

"Have something more to eat," said Cosie.

I opened the chocolate wrapper and broke off a block of chocolate and sucked on it for a long time.

"Would you like some chocolate?" I asked.

"Dogs can't eat chocolate," said Cosie, "It makes us sick," he said. "Anyway, I am full."

"What are we going to do now?" I asked down hearted.

"Why don't you throw me?" suggested Cosie.

"What?" I said in disbelief.

"Throw me," said Cosie.

"What if I miss?" I said.

"We're in a computer game," said Cosie, "and the bird came back when you threw him into the abyss."

"But I can't lose you!" I said.

"Don't over think it," said Cosie. "Just throw me and see what happens."

"And how will I get to you?" I asked.

"You need to take a giant jump from the top of the tower," said Cosie.

I must have looked sceptical.

"You can do it," said Cosie. "I will catch you on the other side.".

I threw Cosie.

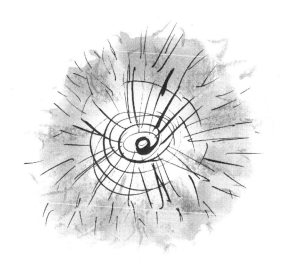

Chapter 5: Finding Digiboy

"I can't hold on," shouted Cosie.

I could hear Cosie's claws scratching on the platform as he tried to hold on.

"I'm coming," I said.

And without thinking, I took a giant leap. My arms were flailing as I flew through the air. Cosie slipped off the platform and started to fall. I reached the platform, but immediately jumped off following Cosie.

"I'm coming," I shouted again.

"Noooo," shouted Cosie.

It was so black and I could not see Cosie. At first my arms were flailing trying to control my fall, then I relaxed waiting for the impact. It didn't come. I landed in what seemed like a cloud cushion. "Cosie," I called out, "are you ok?"

"I'm over here," he said laughing.

"What was that?" I asked.

"Maybe a character test?" said Cosie.

"You demonstrated strength of character, selflessness, friendship and loyalty when you jumped off the platform to follow me," said Cosie. "So, we won that challenge?"

"This is a weird game," I said.

The clouds smelled like marshmallows, taking me back to Halloween when I toasted them with my cousins on the bonfire. I decided to taste them. They tasted like candyfloss. Cosie and I feasted on the candyfloss clouds until we fell through the bottom of the cloud because we had eaten too much! We landed on top of a grassy hill and rolled down to the bottom laughing all the way. We could not stop giggling. My hands were sticky, my face was sticky, and my clothes were sticky. "I bet you my finger will stick to your nose Cosie..." I said laughing.

"Don't you touch my nose," we were both laughing uncontrollably now while I chased Cosie around on the grass. Maybe it was the sugar, or maybe there was something else like laughing gas in the clouds, but we could not stop giggling.

"Your situation isn't all that funny," said a voice from behind us.

We whipped around so fast, Cosie nearly knocked me off my feet.

"Who are you?" we said together.

And then looked at each other and started laughing again.

"Your situation is not really a laughing matter. I have been here for... I'm not really sure now, maybe 3 years... I've stopped counting it's been so long!"

The boy was bigger than me and could not have been much older than me when he arrived if he was now about 12.

"Are you... Digiboy?" I asked slowly, the penny dropping.

"That would be me... the one and only," the boy said with a smirk.

"I was hoping you'd be able to help me get out of here," I said, "but if you are still here, then you haven't cracked it either," I said, the realization dawning on me.

"It's not as bad as all that," said Cosie piping up, cheerful as ever. "There are now three of us."

"A talking dog?" asked Digiboy.

"Yes," we said together without missing a beat and carried on.

"We have a lot of different talents, some food and we are winning," said Cosie.

Now Digiboy started laughing.

"Winning?!?!" "You might think you are, but you are not. The game changes all the time. There are no rules and it is ruthless. I also used to think I was winning, but I am still here!"

"Sounds like you have given up completely," I said, feeling really sad for Digiboy.

"Did I tell you that I have been here for 3 long years?!?!?"

"ALONE!!!!"

"If there is a way in, there has to be a way out," I said logically.

"Well, I haven't found it yet," said Digiboy.

"But there are three heads now," I said, "We can beat this game."

"You need to tell us everything you know," said Cosie in a practical tone.

"Let's walk and look for water, because all that candyfloss has made me really thirsty," I said.

As the word thirsty left my lips, clouds rushed together and torrential rain poured down.

"Water!" I shouted.

"Don't drink it!" said Digiboy, "It's acid rain." "We need to find shelter fast."

We followed Digiboy, who ran into what looked like a wall covered in ivy. Behind the ivy was a cave. We stopped, panting to catch our breath. "You have to get those wet clothes off," he shouted as he started taking his T-shirt off. "The water will burn your skin." I was starting to feel prickles on my skin already. I undressed quickly, but luckily my undies weren't wet!

"Is this where you live?" I asked.

"We need to dry off Cosie," he said.

Cosie was already rolling in the dust, "I'm good," he said jumping up covered in muck.

"This is where I live some of the time. I have a few spots in different levels, and

45

I know some routes between them. I need to go to different games to get different things just to survive."

"That's priority number one, but I haven't managed to crack the code yet to get out."

"How did you end up in the game?" asked Cosie.

"Well," said Digiboy, "I am a coder. I used to spend all my free time coding."

"Me too," I said. "I love coding!"

"But I took it a step too far," he said "I wrote the code for this game."

"You wrote the code for **this game!**" I said, with a mixture of shock and awe.

"Then you know how to get us out!"

"I'm afraid not," said Digiboy. "It is hundreds of thousands of lines of code."

"But you know the structure," I said, "It's **YOUR** code."

"Not anymore," said Digiboy. "I built in artificial intelligence (AI) so that the code would learn and evolve. I also added in random sequences so that each time you played the game would be different."

"It was… I mean *is* very good, and I was selling it to the leaders in gaming…"

Digiboy seemed to drift off.

"So, what happened?" asked Cosie quietly bringing him back.

"Well I assumed that adults were all ethical and honest… and it turns out they are NOT," he said bitterly.

"I had made a deal, and even had a lawyer look over my deal and it was all signed and sealed."

"They put in a condition about beta testing."

"What does that mean?" asked Cosie.

"It means I had to test it one more time before the big launch of the game," I said, hanging on Digiboy's every word.

"But the beta testing version I was testing was just for me," said Digiboy. "They changed something in the code, and after I tested it, I couldn't get out!"

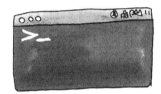

Chapter 6: Finding the Code

"I'm really thirsty," said Cosie.

"We need to find you water right away," said Digiboy.

"Where can we get water that is not contaminated," I asked.

"I call it the river of life," said Digiboy. "You are going to have to trust me… We need to enter the tunnels to get there."

I whimpered at the thought. Digiboy noticed. "I'll take you on the shortest route."

The rain was slowing down. Digiboy explained that they were feeling thirsty because of the candy floss and that they really shouldn't eat it again. I was still only wearing my underwear, so Digiboy gave me his coat. "When we get to the river, we can wash your clothes, just bundle them up for now."

I looked ridiculous in Digiboy's coat as it was too big for me.

I thought Digiboy was **soooo cool!** Even though his clothes were old and tatty, there was still something about him. He was confident, funny and he also really knew his stuff. How could he be so young and such an amazing coder? I wondered briefly whether I was just an avatar in a game, but then I felt my stomach rumble and remembered that I was really stuck in this game.

"Come on, let's get moving, it is a bit of a way through the tunnels", said Digiboy.

Fortunately, these tunnels were underground tunnels that you walked through instead of tumbling, although they were also very, very dark!

I was not a fan of the dark! My sister enjoyed springing out on me at night which made me edgy in the dark. Now I wished she would spring out on me!

I ran my finger along the wall of the tunnel and kept chatting to try to distract myself.

"So, what is your real name?" I asked.

There was a very long pause.

"I don't usually tell people my real name," he said. "But since it is just you and me,"

"and me!" interrupted Cosie.

"and you, sorry Cosie," said Digiboy.

"My name is Oscar."

"My friends call me Digiboy, but I don't mind what you call me."

"I think I'm going to call you **'nincompoop'** for getting us trapped in your game!" I said, with a grin. We both started laughing.

"So, tell me about the game?" I said.

"Well the one we are in is different to the one I designed," said Oscar.

"I want to know about the original game," I said.

Cosie butted in, "Wouldn't we be better off focusing on the new game?"

"Maybe not," I said.

"Oscar only knows what he coded. He doesn't know how it was changed. If we can work through the structure of the code, perhaps we can figure out how it has been corrupted to trap us in here."

"OK, but I have gone through the code a million times in my head and I don't know how they did it," said Oscar.

"Fresh eyes… or imaginary fresh eyes on imaginary code!"

"Well, I suppose we have nothing else to do and it is a long walk."

"So, what is the same?" I asked.

"The overall concepts and levels are all the same."

"I mean, I designed the acid rain and the laughing gas candyfloss clouds. This is how I know what to do and where to go to get fresh water."

"None of these things seem to have changed."

"What has changed?" I asked.

"The tunnels. There are now booby traps that blow up areas and also the tunnels sometimes adjust meaning I can't always get to where I want to go to using a path that worked before."

We arrived at the water and I drank so much water, I thought my stomach might explode. I could barely move. Then I had to bend down to wash my clothes in the stream. This nearly made me sick! After that, I lay down and watched the candy clouds and waited for my clothes to dry a bit.

"So, I have some questions for you and Cosie," said Oscar.

"How did you two end up in this game?"

"I have been coding for as long as I can remember," I said. "At first it was all just fun, you know all the problems set for kids so that we can learn, but I loved it!"

"I coded day and night!"

My dad was always warning me about the dangers of the internet. My mum on the other hand was always encouraging me to code and helping me to figure things out. My mom works as a coder solving big data problems.

"My mom obviously doesn't know what has happened to me, or she would have cracked this by now," I said trailing off.

"You haven't really answered my question…" said Oscar.

"I found your game on the internet and it was free to download."

"What, they are giving it away for free?" exclaimed Oscar.

"Not really, now lots of things are free, but you can buy things in the game, which means they make money."

"I'm not allowed to buy things in games, so I tried to hack the game to make my own one."

"What?"

"Well, I was just going to re-use bits of code to make my own game where I didn't have to buy anything to be able to play."

"What bits of code did you steal?" asked Oscar.

"It's not stealing…" I said, "…just re-using code, it's allowed for open source code."

"It's my code and it's stealing!"

"You sold your code and it's free out on the internet," I said.

"I didn't get any money," said Oscar.

"So what bits did you steal… I mean re-use?" asked Oscar sarcastically.

Before I could answer, a loud explosion blasted in the tunnel ahead. Hot air threw us off our feet.

Cosie shook the dust off himself sending more dust into the air, making us both cough.

"We'll have to go back," said Oscar.

"I can smell food," said Cosie starting to run towards the hot air from the explosion.

"Wait," shouted Oscar.

"It's not safe!" I yelled and ran after Cosie.

Oscar threw up his hands and ran after both of us.

We got to the giant crater that the explosion had created and stopped at the edge. Cosie, being a dog had just run down the crater and up the other side and carried on along the tunnel. This was not as easy for two-legged creatures!

Oscar and I sort of ski-slid down the crater and then scrabbled up the other side.

By the time we had reached the tunnel, we were covered head to toe in dust and Cosie was nowhere to be seen.

"He'll be following the smell," said Oscar seeing the look on my face.

We jogged along the tunnel until we reached a three-way junction.

"I can hear barking," I said.

"... but from which tunnel?" asked Oscar.

"It sounds like the one on the left."

We followed that tunnel for five minutes and ended up back where we had started.

"I thought you knew the tunnels," I said.

" It is the AI. It changes the tunnels all the time, so I have to figure out the route every day!"

We heard Cosie bark again.

We tried the remaining tunnel and this turned out to be a really fast slide. We whooshed down and bumped out the other end onto the grass under a tree.

"Cosie, can you stay in one place please so that we can talk about the code," asked Oscar. We lay down under a tree and relaxed. Cosie put his nose on my lap and closed his eyes. It was warm and reminded me of my dog at home. I looked up into the tree. The fruit hanging off the branches were not like anything I had seen before.

"You can eat these," said Oscar plucking one and tossing it over to me. I bit into the fruit and it tasted like vanilla and strawberry together, but looked like a pear.

"These are amazing!" I said plucking a second off the tree.

"Let's not get distracted, what code bits did you *borrow*?" asked Oscar again.

"I used quite a few," I said.

"Overall, I just grabbed the tunnels, velocity the gravity modules."

"I was making my own designs for the wrapper. I designed basic avatars so that players could make their own characters by choosing different clothes, hair colour etc."

"There were even dogs in my game…"

"Maybe that is why Cosie is in this game?" suggested Oscar.

"Maybe, but all of my avatars are cartoons…"

"…and Cosie seems like a normal dog."

"Cosie can speak! That is not normal," said Oscar.

"I can hear you," said Cosie, opening one eye.

"Well, why don't you tell us how you got into this game?" said Oscar.

"Well I don't really know how I got in," said Cosie.

"Bloop, Bloop, Bloop!"

"What is that?" I asked.

"That is someone changing levels," said Oscar.

"There are others in the game?!?!?!" Cosie and I asked together.

"It seems that you have opened a door."

"What do you mean?" I asked.

"A virtual door," said Oscar.

"It means someone is coming onto our level."

"Do you hear that?"

"Boom! Boom! Boom!"

"Aaaaaaaagh!!!!"

And then !pop! a girl appeared, confused and said:

"Who are you?"

Scared, she picked up a sharp stick and shouted, "Get back!!!!"

Oscar said: "Hello, my name is Oscar, what is yours?"

"Kristina," she said, still pointing the stick towards Oscar.

"Hi Kristina," I said.

"Finn!?!?!" she said, dropping the stick, running towards me, and giving me a giant hug.

"I didn't know what had happened to you!" she said, "It's been days!"

"You look hungry, have one of these," said Oscar, tossing one of the fruits to her.

She caught it with one hand and then looked at it sceptically.

"It is really good," I said.

Kristina sniffed it and slowly bit into it.

"Sweet hybrid genius!!!" she exclaimed.

"This is like strawberry-vanilla ice-cream fruit!"

We ate as much fruit as we could stomach and then filled our pockets with more.

"You shouldn't eat so much fruit or you'll get sick," warned Oscar.

Kristina started to sing.

"When you've eaten too much fruit and you really need to toot!

... Diarrhoea, ... Diarrhoea!"

We were all laughing now as we got up to walk. We walked for hours and hours.

"Why are we walking and where are we going?" asked Kristina.

"We need to get to the computer terminal," said Oscar.

"We need to rest!" I said, leaning against a tree.

"Why do we need to get to the terminal?" asked Kristina.

"So that we can get out," I said.

"Why do you want to get out? asked Kristina.

"I just got here, I don't want to go yet."

"This game is **AWESOME!**"

"Not when you have been here for **3 YEARS!**" said Oscar.

"We need to rest," I said again.

"Yeh," said Kristina and Cosie, and everyone sat down.

Oscar tried to talk to Finn alone…

"If she is trying to persuade us to stay, then she might be part of the code."

"What?" I said.

"We need to be cautious," said Oscar.

"No more talking about coding or the terminal in front of her…"

"…only survival and winning the game levels from now on."

"I can't think straight anymore," I said, as I slid onto the floor with my head in my hands. I was exhausted. I don't remember deciding to go to sleep, but I must have dozed off while trying to think it all through.

I woke up and heard another **pop!** and Jean-Luca appeared.

"Jean-Luca!?!" I shouted, running over to hug him.

"Wait," said Oscar, "you know him too?"

"Yah!!!!" Jean-Luca and I said together.

"Jean-Luca is my best friend!" I said.

"How did you also get into the game?" Oscar asked.

"Finn showed me the game that he was making and when I hadn't seen him for a few days, I started playing the game because I was bored and now here I am!"

said Jean-Luca looking pleased with himself.

"It sounds like your hacked game is a portal into this game, so you have somehow opened the door!" said Oscar.

"We are going to have lots of kids in here soon unless we figure out how to get out and close the portal," I said.

"Bloop, bloop, bloop!"

"That's someone else arriving now!" said Cosie.

"How many people did you give your game to Finn?" asked Oscar.

"Only Kristina, Jean-Luca and ..."

"Kieran!" We all shouted together, running over to give him a hug.

Oscar watched astounded. He had been alone for so long and now he had four friends and a talking dog.

"OK, which of you can code?" asked Oscar.

"We all can!" we answered together.

"We all helped Finn to make the new game," said Kieran.

"Where did you all land in the game?" asked Oscar.

"A floating platform," said Kieran.

"...with lots of computers," said Jean-Luca

"...and tunnels with buttons," said Kristina.

"I think we all arrived in the same place," I said.

"That sounds like the control centre," said Oscar.

"That's where we will be able to edit the code."

"If that's the way in, then maybe that's the way out?" said Kieran.

"But it would be impossible to climb those tunnels!" I said remembering how badly my clothes were ripped.

"I don't think we need to climb the tunnels, I think we just need to edit the code at the terminal," said Oscar.

"Well we can't go back the way we came," said Cosie "unless you have a flying machine!"

"Yes, it is pretty much impossible to get back to the control centre directly," said Oscar.

"… but I made a level in the game where you have to fix code to win the level,"

"There is a computer terminal there," said Oscar.

"Well that's where we have to go then," I said.

"The problem is, that level is protected by hot lava and I haven't figured out a way to get across to the terminal," said Oscar.

"**COOL!**" said Kristina, who was always up for an adventure.

"Let's go," she said jumping to her feet.

"**Whoa!**" said Oscar. "We need to plan first."

"What do we need to plan?" said Kristina impatiently.

"We need provisions... fresh water, food and rest," said Kieran who was always good at organising provisions when we went on trips.

"Once we go down this route, there is no turning back!" said Oscar.

"The game is ruthless, non-stop and we may not make it to the other side," said Oscar.

Kieran had started to pace up and down.

"Since you can't sit still, you can go get the water from the river of life," said Oscar.

"I don't think we should split up," I said.

"I'll go," said Kieran.

"I'll take Cosie and I'll be back in no time."

Cosie who had been sleeping, raised an ear and yawned.

"What are we doing now?" asked Cosie.

"You and I are going to fetch water," said Kieran.

"I'm right behind you," said Cosie, going back to sleep.

"But how will you find your way back to us," I said.

"I have a penknife," said Kieran.

"I can carve arrows into the tunnels to show which way we need to go."

"I will make a mark every 20 metres," said Kieran. "Come on Cosie, let's go."

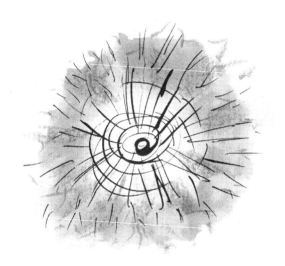

Chapter 7: Fetching water

Kristina, Jean-Luca and I lay back relaxing, while I asked Oscar hundreds of questions about the game. The biggest problem it seemed was that we did not know how to get to the lava field which was the last level. Oscar also had no idea about how to survive the hot lava. We would have to figure that out once we got there. Until then, we would need to focus on getting there.

Meanwhile, Kieran and Cosie were on their own new adventure to get water. Kieran had not met the beast or experienced acid rain or any of the other problems that Finn had had. Kieran started making the markings on the tunnels as they walked while Cosie led the way.

"I am sure I know the way back to the river," said Cosie.

Kieran had made at least 30 marks on the tunnel and was starting to get tired.

"Are we there yet?" asked Kieran.

Just as he said it, Cosie started to run. Kieran followed, forgetting about the wall markings. They could hear the water rushing over the stones.

They drank their fill from the river and then set about trying to find something to carry the water in. There were no water bottles, but there were lots of coconuts on the floor. Kieran used a stick to make some holes and drained out the coconut milk and filled them with water. He laid them out with the holes up next to the tree with the delicious fruit. He tied six unopened coconuts to Cosie's back using vines that he found. He didn't mind drinking coconut milk and they could also eat the coconut flesh. Then he filled his pockets with fruit and his arms with coconuts filled with water.

"That should be enough," said Cosie.

"We can always come back if we need more," said Kieran as they headed back towards the tunnels.

"Which one is it?" asked Cosie.

"I'm not sure," said Kieran, "I ran after you when you took off towards the water."

"You were supposed to mark which one," said Cosie.

"I was trying not to lose you," said Kieran.

"No problem, I think I should be able to pick up your scent," said Cosie.

"Can you step back a bit so that I can't smell you?" asked Cosie, heading towards the first tunnel opening.

"I think that is the strangest thing anyone has ever asked me," said Kieran. "But then I am talking to a dog... and talking to myself..."

"Not a good sign!" said Cosie.

"It's this one!" he said, pointing with his nose.

They trundled back up the tunnel at a steady pace and found the first marker. As they reached the 6th marker, a large robot entered from a side tunnel and blocked their path. The robot started moving toward Kieran and Cosie fast.

Cosie shouted, "ruuunnn!!!!"

Kieran did not run. He seemed to freeze on the spot.

Cosie shouted again "ruuuunnn!!!"

Kieran did not move.

"Oh, come on!" said Cosie running back to fetch Kieran.

As Cosie arrived back, Kieran grabbed a coconut from Cosie's back and fired it at the robot. This only seemed to anger the bot.

Kieran grabbed another coconut and fired it at the robot's shoulder and its arm fell off with sparks flying everywhere.

This really angered the bot! It started running full tilt at Kieran and Cosie. Kieran loved playing ball and spent a lot of time in the garden playing catch. He stood his ground, grabbed another coconut and wound it up and threw it straight at the bot's head. This knocked its head straight off! There were more sparks and fizzing and the robot keeled over, falling to the ground with a crash!

"Wooohoo!!!" shouted Cosie.

"Bull's eye!" said Kieran.

"or rather robot eye," said Cosie, and they both started laughing.

"High five!" shouted Kieran and then realised he was talking to a dog, lowering his hand.

They collected up the remaining coconuts securing them to Cosie again, stepped over the sparking robot and walked on.

When they returned, everyone else was sleeping. They sat down to rest and fell into a deep, deep sleep.

Chapter 8: Jean-Luca

We woke up refreshed and ready for the next challenge. When Kieran woke up, Kristina, Jean-Luca, Oscar and I were already eating fruit and discussing the next plan. The mission was to find the hot lava field. It sounded way too dangerous, but that is what we were going to do! Oscar had an idea about how to get to the lava field.

"The tunnels are underground and the lava field is above ground, so we need to go up," said Oscar.

"How do we do that?" asked Jean-Luca.

Just then, we heard a rumble.

"Oh no" said Oscar, "Ruuuuunnn!"

We all ran for our lives, not thinking where we were going, or what we were running from, just running as fast as we could. My chest was burning, but I didn't look back, I just followed Oscar. When we finally reached sunlight, we all spilt out of the tunnel and collapsed in a heap. The rumble was a tidal wave flushing the tunnels, the water splashed out the top of the tunnel, like a blowhole and then sucked back in. Oscar had seen this before and so he knew what the sound meant, which is why he told us to run. If we hadn't run at that moment, we would have all drowned. I looked around.

Jean-Luca was not there!

"Noooooo!!!!" I shouted, rushing over and looking into the tunnel. The water was draining back quickly like it was being sucked away.

"Jean-Luca!" I shouted.

"Jean-Luca!"

Looking into the tunnel full of water, I knew there was no hope.

Nobody else said anything. There was nothing to say. My chest ached from running and from deep, deep sadness. My friend was gone, and there was no going back into the tunnels to look for him. They were flooded. I sank to my knees. Tears rolled down my cheeks. Kristina and Kieran tried to comfort me, but they were also distraught.

"It's just a game..." said Kristina trailing off, tears rolling down her cheeks as well.

"I'm sure he's fine," said Kieran throwing an arm around my shoulder, but I could see the pain in his face.

Neither of them sounded convinced by their own words. Cosie came and sat next to me, so close he was nearly on top of me. He didn't move at all, just sat leaning on me.

Oscar did not say anything. The air felt thick, like it was too hard to breathe or speak. I felt like there was a really heavy weight on my shoulders pushing me into the ground, holding me there on the spot.

After a while, Oscar said, "we have to keep moving."

"We can't leave my friend behind," I said.

"There's nothing else we can do for him," said Oscar.

"He is gone!"

The words sounded so final. I couldn't help feeling it was all my fault. If I hadn't coded the video game and given it to my friends, Jean-Luca wouldn't be gone.

I got up and started putting one foot in front of the other again. Cosie stayed right by my side while we walked. The tears rolled down my face and splashed onto the floor. Kristina put her arm around my shoulders as we walked. At first, she said nothing. After a while when the tears had slowed down, she said, "I'm not sure what has happened to Jean-Luca, but I think the best thing we can do is to beat this game and get out."

"But what if Jean-Luca really is dead?" I said, my voice cracking.

"That's not normally how computer games work," said Kristina.

"This is not a normal game," I said.

"It's more likely that he has three lives and he's landed back at the beginning of the level or the start of the game," said Kristina.

"If you could die to get out of the game, then Oscar could have just died to go home," said Kieran. "So, it is most likely Jean-Luca is OK, just somewhere else in the game."

"He knows what we are planning, so I'm sure he will figure out how to reconnect with us," said Kristina.

"We can't beat this game without you," said Kieran.

"And you can't think straight when you are so upset," said Kristina.

I took a deep breath and let it out slowly counting to ten as I went. I did this again and then Kristina gave me a coconut to have a drink.

Chapter 9: Hot Lava

We were one step closer to finding the volcano. We were out of the tunnels, but now there were new challenges.

"The volcano is on higher ground, so we need to move through that jungle," said Oscar pointing to the dense forest.

"An active volcano will have destroyed any trees or grass nearby," said Kieran.

"Stay alert!" said Oscar.

"I've been in this jungle before and there are lots of dangers."

We all started looking around at the same time. There was a humming sound, but it was not clear where it was coming from. The sky started to darken. The sound was high-pitched and intense! Instinctively, we all started to crouch down.

"Lie down!" shouted Kristina." They're cicadas!"

"They won't harm us, but you have to lay low!" Kristina loved watching nature videos and knew about all sorts of creatures, but this was a video game and so nature's rules no longer applied. They could just as easily be giant kid eating cicadas!

We all piled on top of each other and waited for the cicadas to pass. Some landed and got caught in our hair, but they did not bite or hurt anyone. "What was the point of that?" asked Kieran. "Just to scare us, I think," said Kristina. "Some people really don't like insects."

"Stand still," she shouted at Kieran.

We all spun around. There was a giant spider on Kieran's back.

It was too late, Kieran was already running and trying to hit the spider. It jumped onto his face and sunk its mandibles into his cheek. Kristina ran after him and tried to squeeze the poison out of his wound, but immediately his face started to swell.

"Let's keep moving," Oscar said.

I was about to start arguing that we needed to rest and look after Kieran when Oscar said: "We need to get out of this game before that poison takes effect."

Kristina took Kieran's pen knife and went over to one of the trees. She cut a deep hole into the bark and collected up some sap.

"What are you doing?" I asked.

"I'm making a treatment that will draw the poison out of Kieran's cheek," she said, packing it onto his face.

"Swinging vines," said Oscar. "These will get us out of the forest quick."

"OK, let's go, before the poison kicks in," said Kristina.

"We're going that way," said Oscar pointing to a hill where they could see smoke.

"Stay high, let's go!"

We started to swing between the trees for what seemed like forever, and then suddenly, the trees thinned and we ran out of vines and trees. We would have to hike the rest of the way. The bush was thick and thorny. We pushed on, ripping our clothes and scratching our skin.

"I could really use a break," said Kieran.

His face was very, very swollen and angry looking.

"Let's have some water and something to eat," I said.

We were close enough now that we could already feel the heat from the volcano and the vegetation had started to die off because of it.

We were heading for the boulder fields.

Kristina whispered in my ear. "We need to get Kieran some help soon."

"OK, that's enough of a break, we've got to keep moving," I said.

Everyone groaned a bit, but they got up and started moving towards the volcano.

Kieran was starting to hallucinate. He was swatting flies that weren't there and shouting about nothing. We tried to shepherd him towards the volcano. He was shouting at us that we were all trying to get him. He was becoming very difficult to manage. Just then the earth started to shake which didn't help. "The volcano is going to erupt," shouted Oscar.

There was nothing we could do except try to avoid the falling rocks. The earth started to crack and we could see the orange lava flowing below the surface.

"Stick together," I shouted in between the loud cracking noises.

Kieran started running away from us looking over his shoulder as if someone was chasing him.

"He's hallucinating again," said Kristina, going after him.

He was looking over his shoulder running away from an imaginary monster that was not there.

"Wait," shouted Kristina, "Nothing's chasing you."

"Nooooooo," she cried, as Kieran fell into a crack and disappeared in the lava flow.

We all peered over the edge. Kieran was gone. All we could see was the fast-flowing boiling lava.

"I can't just keep going!" I said.

"We have to keep going," said Oscar.

"At all costs?" I said, "Kieran was my friend,"

"He was my friend too," said Kristina, a tear rolling down her cheek. "The ground is unstable, we need to move."

The ground started to shake again.

"Move!" shouted Oscar.

"Head for the top!"

We all started hopping between rocky islands avoiding the rivers of lava flowing down the mountain. The air was thick with smoke.

"This doesn't seem like such a good idea," I said.

"Stay low and follow Cosie," said Oscar.

We got to the lava field. It was bigger than I had expected and really hot. Our feet were burning hot, and the sweat was pouring off all of us.

"This is it," said Oscar.

"This is impossible!" I said. "There is no way we can get across this!"

"There is… see that swing bridge over there," said Oscar pointing to an old wooden swing bridge.

"It doesn't look strong enough," I said.

"I'll go first and test it," said Cosie.

"No," I said. "I can't lose you too!"

"I'm the lightest," said Cosie. "It has to be me."

"I'm going," said Cosie, nudging me with his nose.

I ruffled his fur and hugged him tight.

He took the first cautious steps. The bridge creaked. Cosie looked back and we all held our breath.

He carried on cautiously and then rocketed across at full speed.

"OK, safe enough for a dog, who's next?" asked Oscar.

"I'll go," said Kristina.

Before we could get into extended goodbyes, Kristina was running over the bridge.

"OK Finn, you're next..." said Oscar.

I decided that running was best. I took the first cautious step and then bolted across the bridge. Only Oscar was left now. He was a bit older and always seemed to be a little braver than the rest of us... Not this time though, he hesitated not wanting to run.

"Come on!" we shouted together gesturing to Oscar to come over. The ground started to shake again and the lava was boiling. Oscar realizing it was his last chance started to sprint over the bridge. The metal railings started to creak and melt and the bridge snapped and started to swing.

"Hold on Oscar!" I shouted.

The bridge swung to the side and Oscar who had clung on now was yelling, but we could not hear what he was saying.

I looked over the edge and saw that had started climbing up the wooden slats that used be the bridge. The slats had made the perfect ladder!

When he got to the top, we grabbed his
hands and swung him over the edge.
Oscar's hands were badly burned from
the boiling hot metal railings.

"We need to get away from this heat," said Kristina passing around the last of the coconuts. "That's where we are going," said Oscar pointing higher on the mountain. "The exit is up in the cave on the side of the mountain over there. It should be cooler, you can see there are some trees there, so it can't be too hot."

"There is no way I will be able to climb with my blistered hands!," said Oscar. "They are so sore!" he said, tears filling his eyes. I ripped some of my shirt off, poured the last of the water onto the cloth and wrapped it around Oscar's hands gently to cool them down.

"We'll figure it out together," I said as we started to walk towards the cave.

Thankfully, the walk was shorter than it seemed when we first looked at it and there was only one tricky bit that we needed to climb. We hauled Oscar up the bit that we had to climb since his hands were so bad. Kristina gave him a boost while I pulled his arms, trying to avoid touching his hands. We rolled over exhausted at the top. We had now run out of food and water and were completely spent, but we had reached the cave.

Chapter 10: Cracking the Code

"OK Oscar, what do we do here?" asked Kristina examining the door that looked impenetrable.

"I don't know," said Oscar. "I didn't code this door."

"Did you code this Finn?" asked Oscar.

"I don't think any of my code is in this game... I think my game just acted as a portal to get us into yours," I said.

"They must have put this in to keep you in the game if you got this far," I said.

Kristina ran her hands around the edge of the door.

"It is completely sealed and there is no handle," she said.

She was examining it closely looking at every centimetre.

"It looks like some of these wooden panels might be able to move," she said trying to slide one.

I went over to help her push.

"It's like a giant puzzle box," said Kristina.

"What do you mean?" asked Oscar.

"The ones where you have to push the wood in different ways to open the box," said Kristina.

"I have never had one of those," said Oscar.

"My parents give me one every Christmas," said Kristina, "Help me slide this big one."

Oscar and I helped Kristina slide the wooden slats in different directions, but after an hour, we still had not solved the puzzle.

Kristina wasn't giving up. She loved puzzles.

"There are only so many different combinations," she said, still focused on the door. "We just have to try them all."

She started at the bottom again and slowly moved the wood, gently until she felt the wood settle in a new position. She did that for all of them with her cheek against each plank listening and feeling the vibrations with her cheek.

Oscar and I just watched as she worked. She didn't get frustrated, just carried on working.

"I have never seen anyone so focused and persistent," said Oscar.

"That's it!" I shouted. "You got it!"

Kristina looked surprised. The door was still closed.

Behind her and next to me, a small console had lowered itself down with a keyboard.

"OK," I said pushing up my sleeves. "I got this."

"We might only have three tries," said Oscar.

"You know these guys, Oscar," I said.

"Not really…" said Oscar, "I only met them a few times."

"You may know more than you think about them," I said.

"Just say the first things that come to your mind when you think about them."

"Crooks… thieves… liars!" said Oscar through gritted teeth.

"No, not that," I said.

"Did they tell you about things they liked, personal things?"

Think back to when you had good interactions with them in the beginning," I probed.

"Oh, I don't know."

"Kristina, you're super good at hacking things... help us out here," I said.

"Where were they from?" asked Kristina.

"The one guy was from Kent, and the other guy was from somewhere in the south of England. He kept going on about how beautiful the New Forest was."

"That's good," said Kristina.

"...any kids?" asked Kristina.

"No-one would marry those twits!!!" said Oscar.

"This is not going to work if you get all angry," said Kristina. "Concentrate!"

"Just chill, Oscar," I said, "we're getting out."

"Any pets?" asked Kristina, carrying on in a formal business-like manner.

"He talked about walking his dog in that forest," said Oscar.

"Now this is seriously important," said Kristina.

"What is his dog's name?"

Oscar closed his eyes.

"He said it, but I can't remember," said Oscar.

"Think back to the start of the conversation. Was he talking about walking the dog in the forest?"

"No, he was talking about taking the dog to the vet."

"He genuinely seemed to care about the dog."

"People give their dogs silly names sometimes," said Kristina.

"Did you think the dog's name was a good name or a silly name?"

"I've got it," said Oscar.

"His dog's name was 'Hund'!"

"I thought this was particularly silly because 'hund' means dog in German, so it is like calling your dog 'dog'!"

"Is the guy German?" I asked.

"No. I don't think so. He didn't have a German accent."

"What were their names?" asked Kristina carrying on.

"John and Neill," said Oscar.

"Surnames?"

"Mmmm… John….Jackson, I think."

"and Neill... I can't remember..."

"Do you remember anything about his surname?" asked Kristina.

"His surname was a first name..."

"Neill..." Oscar was looking up to the sky trying to remember Neill's second name.

"Neill Hughes." "That's it."

"Any chance you know their birthdays?" asked Kristina.

"Yes," said Oscar.

Kristina had not expected that reply.

"Really!?!?" "What is it?"

"Neill's birthday is the first of April 2000." "He was bragging about being born on April fool's day in the year 2000."

"What about John?" asked Kristina.

"They took me out to dinner on John's birthday."

"What day was that?" asked Kristina.

"That was the day before we signed the deal. The 3rd of October…." Oscar trailed off.

"Was that the day you signed the deal or was that his birthday?" asked Kristina still in a business-like mode.

"The 3rd of October was the day we signed," said Oscar. "His birthday is the 2nd of October."

"How old was he that year?" asked Kristina.

"He was 22 that year," said Oscar.

"What year did you sign the deal?" asked Kristina.

"It was 2018," said Oscar.

"That means he was born in 1996," I said.

"Who was the brains behind the operation?" I asked, taking over.

"What do you mean?" asked Oscar.

"Which one of them could code?" asked Kristina.

"The guy with the dog," said Oscar.

"Which one had the dog?" asked Kristina.

"Neill," said Oscar.

"Let's try 'Hund01042000'," I said.

"There are too many numbers," said Kristina.

"What about 'Hund010400'," I said.

A loud beep told us that it hadn't worked.

"We probably only have 3 goes," said Kristina.

"Try 'Hund1400'" I said.

"Beeeeeeep!"

"Last try," said Kristina.

"What do you think will happen if we get it wrong?" said Kristina

"Let's not think about that..." I said.

"What about putting an exclamation mark at the end," said Oscar.

Kristina typed in 'Hund010400!'

I held my breath and she pressed enter...

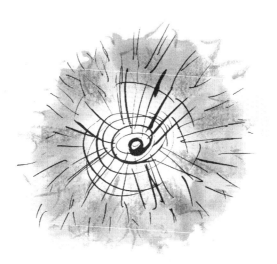

Chapter 11: Game Changer

The door clicked, opened and we were all sucked into a vortex.

"AAAAAAGHH!!!"

"Are we dying?" shouted Kristina.

No one could hear her above the noise of rushing air as we spun around. It felt like we were in a tornado. We slammed into the platform bumping and rolling. The impact was so strong that I nearly rolled off the side. I vomited over the edge, then stood up swaying and feeling sick.

"Jean-Luca!, Kieran!" I said, a smile creeping onto my face. They ran over and hugged me. I was a bit unsteady but was very happy to see them. Kristina came over and we all had a big group hug with Cosie barking and jumping around us.

"The terminal," said Oscar, focused on the central computer. He ran his fingers over the carving of Digiboy that he had etched when he had first arrived.

I moved quickly to the terminal control panel.

"Find the tunnel bit in the code," said Oscar.

"How am I meant to do that, there are millions of lines of code," I said.

"You need to find the hashed out lines of code," said Kristina.

I used control plus 'F' for 'find' and searched for the word 'tunnel'".

"Nothing," I said dejected.

"What other words can we use for the tunnels?"

"I used 'supertubes' in my hash lines," said Oscar walking back over.

I entered: Control + 'F' and then 'supertubes'

… and there it was, the code for the tunnels.

"Woohoo!" shouted Kristina.

"OK, so now we need to flatten them all so that we don't have to climb them."

"Make all Y-co-ordinates 'zero'," said Oscar.

"That is so clever," I said.

"Why don't we make the x and z -co-ordinates zero as well, that way, the tunnels will turn into a direct entrance to the platform," said Kristina.

"…and we won't have to do any more walking!" Cosie chimed in.

"Excellent idea!" I said.

"Before we do that, we need to also set a self-destruct sequence so that they can't trap anyone else in this game," said Oscar.

"We need to do something to make sure that the self-destruct only works after we are out of the game," said Kristina stating the obvious.

"What about if we make a loop that just sends people back to the front screen of the game," I said.

"What do you mean?" asked Oscar.

"I mean a loop that keeps returning them to the beginning, effectively not allowing them to enter the game," I said.

"But how will we make sure Neill and John don't edit it out?"

"We just need to add in some random code that will insert in different places all over the game code," said Kristina.

"That way it will be in a different place every time they look."

"But they will have another clean copy on their server.

"We need to take the server down."

"We can't take it down while we are in the game.."

"We don't even know what the server is."

"Type in 'hostname'," said Oscar.

"Why?" I asked.

"That will tell us the name of this terminal and we will be able to shut it down when we are out," said Oscar.

"OK, got it," I said. "Let's get out!"

In a separate window, the code was scrolling really fast. This was a really dangerous manoeuvre, trying to edit the code while it was running, but it was our only option.

I shouted:

"Ready everyone?"

Oscar seemed frozen.

"5, 4, 3….

2, 1…"

I pressed enter.

The tunnels slammed together with a loud

"BANG!!!"

Where there used to be lots of tunnels entering the platform, there was just one black hole left.

"Let's do this together," said Kristina.

We held hands and stepped into the darkness!

Chapter 12: Into the light

As we fell through the air, we were all pulled apart. I felt a strong gravitational pull as well as something pushing against my back. There was a prickly feeling in my arm and a different beeping sound.

"beep... beep... beep... beep..."

It kept on going, not like the sound for level change in a game. I also heard:

"drip… drip… drip…"

I opened my eyes and blinked into bright light again. I was lying on my back and the light hurt my eyes, making me wonder whether I was back in the game again. I turned away from the light and saw what was making the dripping sound. There was a bag of liquid next to me and it was connected to a tube that was connected to my arm!

I hated needles! I started to wriggle around trying to sit up and get the needle out of my arm.

A nurse rushed in.

"Take it easy, sweetheart," she said trying to calm me down.

"Take it out," I said trying to get the tube out of my arm.

"Take it easy," she said again.

In the other beds, Oscar, and Kristina were also waking up and trying to sit up.

"What is going on?" she exclaimed hitting the red button and calling for help.

Cosie started to bark. The nurse was confused...

"What is that dog doing in here?" she said.

"He is my dog!" I said loud and clear.

"We can't have dogs in the hospital," she said.

"You can't take him out of here... he's my dog," I said again.

My parents walked in with Kristina's parents close behind them.

They raced over and hugged us. All the parents were crying.

"We thought we had lost you!" said Kristina's mom.

Where are Jean-Luca and Kieran, asked Kristina sounding a bit groggy.

They're in the room next door.

Jean-Luca and Kieran rushed in babbling excitedly about all the things that had happened.

I immediately realised that we needed to get rid of the adults so that we could close down the game.

"Could you go and get us some chocolate and drinks," I asked my parents to try to get them all out of the room.

"Why don't you go get some coffee for everyone," said Kristina to her parents, "we're OK," she said reassuringly.

Oscar was watching, rubbing his eyes as the nurse checked his heart rate.

"Where are Oscar's parents?" I asked.

"Oscar has been asleep for more than 3 years," said the nurse. They usually visit in the evenings. I am going to call them now.

As the nurse left, Oscar grabbed the laptop next to his bed and started tapping. He checked he was connected to the internet and then went to the command line terminal. He tapped in the server name and logged on using the same user password 'Hund010400!'

He searched for the game code and entered the random return to the start repeating sequence. He logged off and tried to find the game online.

"Don't enter the game again," I said.

"It's OK," said Oscar.

"No one can enter the game anymore."

Oscar slammed the laptop shut as he saw his parents walking in. Tears were rolling down their cheeks as they hugged Oscar.

"The doctors have never seen a case like yours," said his mum.

"They thought it was a virus that they just could not identify."

What they did not know was that it was more like a computer virus that had Oscar in its grips.

The nurse came in.

"The children need to rest," she said.

"Everyone back in bed," she instructed.

".. and that dog needs to go!" she said in a stern voice.

"Mom and Dad, this is Cosie," I said.

"He needs to come home with us."

My parents did not argue. They were so happy I was awake.

Cosie barked and trotted off next to my Mom. I was sure I saw Cosie wink as he left the room.

The end.

Book 4 in the Adventures of Finn O'Shea series -coming soon

The Mystery Code

ISBN: 978-1-7399835-4-3

Chapter 1: Gone without a trace

From one day to the next, she was gone! Once we all realised no teacher was coming, we all erupted into unrestrained giddiness, throwing paper planes and making a racket until the teacher next door called the principal. Her knock on the board was enough to get Kieran down off his desk, sitting down as if nothing had happened. The class gave out a collective sigh as the fun was instantaneously ended. The principal looked worried though, unsure as to why Mrs O'Keefe was not there.

"This is really not like her," she mumbled under her breath and then sat down at Mrs O'Keefe's desk.

"What page are you on, Kristina?"

"Page 64," Kristina said quickly. She knew this was no time for joking around.

The next day, the same thing. No Mrs O'Keefe!

Mrs O'Keefe was our favourite teacher, and we were starting to get worried. The look on the principal's face told us that she was not just off sick.

There was no explanation given at all. When we asked where Mrs O'Keefe was, she just said, "She won't be back for a while, get out your books."

There was a gloomy feel in the class. Everyone knew something was wrong.

The principal and substitute teachers were nothing like Mrs O'Keefe. She was fun and always joking with us. She brought our lessons to life. Her catchphrase was: *'Let's just do it!'* Whenever she said these words, we knew the fun was about to begin. If at all possible her lessons were in the yard. There we had watched so many experiments gone wrong that I thought she did it on purpose just to make us laugh before showing us how to do it properly. We loved her!

...and now she was gone!

Other books by Marian Brennan

Book 1: The Inventions of Finn O'Shea
ISBN: 979-8566652085

Book 2: Astro Fiasco
ISBN: 978-1739983505

Book 3: Digiboy
ISBN: 978-1739983536

Book 4: The Mystery Code (coming soon)
ISBN: 978-1739983543

German Translations

Buch 1: Der Erfinder
ISBN: 978-1739983598

About the author

Prof. Marian Brennan is both a scientist and a writer living in Wicklow in Ireland. After completing a degree in science, she moved to Dublin to do a PhD. She is passionate about science and storytelling. Her children's novels are fun and exciting and written to spark curiosity and inspire young children.

For updates on new releases:

website: www.marianbrennan.com

Twitter: @marianbrennan

Instagram: @marianbrennan_phd

Printed in Great Britain
by Amazon